First Hardcover Edition, December 2015 10 9 8 7 6 5 4 3 2 1
978-1-4847-1420-1
F383-2370-2-15261

Library of Congress Control Number: 2015938614

Printed in China

Visit www.disneybooks.com

Disney Doc McStuffins

Cuddle Me, Lambie

Adapted by Sheila Sweeny Higginson
Based on the episode "A Day Without Cuddles!,"
written by Jennifer Hamburg
for the series created by Chris Nee
Illustrated by Mike Wall

Disney PRESS
Los Angeles • New York

Doc McStuffins had just finished making her bed when she heard a strange sound.

"Seven... eight... nine... ten!" Lambie huffed as she finished her cuddle-ups. "You do remember what today is, Doc, don't you?"

"Of course!" Doc replied. "It's **Cuddle Day**!"
"INTERNATIONAL Cuddle Day,"
said Lambie, correcting her.

Lambie wasn't the only one getting ready for the Cuddle Day celebration. In the McStuffins kitchen, Dad was gathering ingredients. The cuddle cake making was about to begin.

"Happy Cuddle Day!"
Doc greeted him.
"And a happy Cuddle Day to you, Doc!"
he replied.
Then Dad leaned in and gave Lambie an
extra-big cuddle.

Donny heard the Cuddle Day commotion and raced
into the kitchen.
   "Can I help?" he asked.
   "Sure," said Doc. "You can add the flour."

Donny poured flour into the bowl. Then he poured in
some more flour . . . and some more . . . and some more. . . .
"I think that's enough, Donny," Dad said, laughing.
Donny plopped the bag on the table.

THUNK!

And then a cloud
of flour floated over
Lambie.

Dad mixed up the batter and poured it onto the griddle. It was time to watch him make some cuddle cake magic!

FLIP!

FLOP!

Dad flipped the cakes onto Doc's and Donny's plates.

Then he cut them into
heart shapes and sprinkled
blueberries on top.

"Best cuddle cakes ever!"
Doc cheered.

Doc and Donny gobbled up their delicious cuddle cakes.
Then Dad took Donny to his playdate.
"Doc, Mom's working in her office if you need her," Dad called.

"Thanks!" Doc said. "Lambie and I are off to the clinic for the **big** Cuddle **Day** celebration."

Lambie hopped into her cuddle booth and flipped the sign around.

"So beautiful," Lambie sighed. "So many cuddly memories. The cuddle booth is now open for cuddles."

Stuffy, Chilly, Hallie, Bronty, and Sir Kirby rushed to line up for a cuddle. Even the Wicked King tried to get in line—in the wrong spot!

"Hey, no cutsies!" Stuffy reminded the Wicked King.

"Oh, beansicles!" the Wicked King huffed.

"ACHOO!"

Lambie sneezed.

"Lambie, maybe you should come back to the
checkup room for a minute," Doc suggested.
"We can find out why you're sneezing so much."

Lambie's eyes looked good, and so did her nose,
but when she had to open wide and say, "Ahhh!"
a giant *ACHOO!* snuck out instead!

"ACHOO!"

Doc used her reflex hammer to gently tap Lambie's knee.
Lambie's woolly leg kicked forward, sending a puff of flour
into the air.

"Hmmm," Doc said. "Looks like flour."

Doc knew exactly what the problem was.
"Lambie, you must have gotten flour on you when
we were mixing the ingredients for cuddle cakes,"
Doc explained. "You have a case of Flour-tosis.
The flour is what's making you sneeze."

Then Doc gave Lambie the really bad news: until Dad got home and washed the flour out, Lambie wouldn't be able to cuddle. If she did, she could spread Flour-tosis to the other toys.

"I can't cuddle on Cuddle Day?" Lambie sniffed. "This is awful."

Doc was all set to cancel Cuddle Day, but Lambie wouldn't have it. Cuddle Day had to go on! Lambie gathered her toy friends around her.

"This year, I've decided it's time to train other toys in the art of cuddle," Lambie proclaimed. "So today the cuddle booth will be manned by . . ."

"Me, Lambie, pick me!" Stuffy yelled. "Me! Me! Me! Please!"

Since Stuffy said "please,"
he got to be the first in the
cuddle booth.

The toys lined up again,
but Stuffy's dragon-sized
hugs were a lot squeezier
than Lambie's cute cuddles.
The toys started to ask
questions.

"Lambie, I think the toys are wondering why you aren't giving cuddles," Doc whispered. "Maybe you should say something."

"I just want to thank everyone for the wonderful celebration today," Lambie told her friends. "And I'd love to give cuddles to each and every one of you . . .

but how about some high fives instead?"

Stuffy had heard enough. He was determined to get to the bottom of the non-cuddling Lambie mystery.

"Lambie, it's International Cuddle Day and you haven't given one cuddle all day," he said. "So what's going on?"

"Do you want to tell them?" Doc asked.
"Or should I?"

"Oh, all right," Lambie sighed. "I have Flour-tosis!"
"I knew it!" Stuffy said. "And yet I have no idea what that is."
Doc explained that it meant Lambie was covered in flour and couldn't give any cuddles.

"So you're telling us . . . no cuddles on Cuddle Day?" Chilly asked.
"I really wanted to make today special for you all," Lambie said
sadly. "But now International Cuddle Day is ruined!"

Just then, Doc heard a car pulling into the driveway.

"Dad's home!" she said excitedly. "Now we can wash you and get the flour out, Lambie!"

Later Dad poked his head into Doc's room. "Did somebody call for a fluffy, clean, flour-free Lambie?" he asked as he held out Doc's toy.

When Dad left, Doc used her
stethoscope to bring her toys to life.
"Did it work, Doc?" Lambie
wondered. "Is my Flour-tosis gone?"

Doc fluffed up Lambie's wool.
Not a speck of flour in sight!

"I'm so happy I could . . .

CUDDLE!"

Lambie cheered.

"You can," Doc agreed. "And, Lambie,
I was proud of you today. You were a true
friend to the other toys. You didn't want
to get them sick, so you didn't cuddle,
even though you wanted to."

"Is it still Cuddle Day?" Lambie asked.
"Did I miss it?"

Through the window, Doc could see that the sun hadn't set yet. It was still Cuddle Day, and there was plenty of time for cuddles for everyone—

the best kind of cuddles, too:
cuddles from Lambie!